GOOD TO BE GREEN

Don't Waste Your Food

Written by DEBORAH CHANCELLOR
Illustrated by DIANE EWEN

CRABTREE
PUBLISHING COMPANY
WWW.CRABTREEBOOKS.COM

Before, During, and After Reading Prompts

Activate Prior Knowledge and Make Predictions

Read the title of the book to the children and look at the illustrations. Ask children what they think the book may be about. Ask them questions related to the title, such as:

- Which foods do you like to eat? Which foods are not your favorite?
- Do you have food left at meal time? What do you think happens to it?

During Reading

Stop at various points during reading and ask children questions related to the story:

- What does Dad do with Amara's leftovers? (see pages 7–11)
- What kind of food goes in the compost bin? What is compost used for? (see pages 10–13)
- Why do Dad and Amara plan their meals? (see pages 16–17)

- Why does Amara buy fruit from local farms? (see pages 18–21)
- Why do Amara and her dad decide to eat less meat? (see pages 22–23)

After Reading

Look at the information panels, then talk together about air pollution. Ask children the following prompting questions:

- What gas do cows make, and why is this bad for the planet? (see page 23)
- Some foods travel long distances from farm to plate. Is this a good thing? (see page 21)
- What happens to food when we throw it away? (see page 15)
- How can you help reduce food waste? (see pages 17 and 25)

Do the Quiz together (see pages 28–29). Refer back to the information panels to find answers.

Crabtree Publishing Company

www.crabtreebooks.com   1-800-387-7650

Published in Canada
Crabtree Publishing
616 Welland Ave.
St. Catharines, Ontario
L2M 5V6

Published in the United States
Crabtree Publishing
PMB 59051
350 Fifth Avenue, 59th Floor
New York, New York 10118

First published in 2019 by Wayland (an imprint of Hachette Children's Group, part of Hodder and Stoughton)
Copyright © Hodder and Stoughton, 2019

Author: Deborah Chancellor
Illustrator: Diane Ewen
Editorial Director: Kathy Middleton
Editors: Sarah Peutrill, Ellen Rodger
Designer: Cathryn Gilbert
Print and production coordinator: Katherine Berti

Printed in the U.S.A./122019/CG20191101

Library and Archives Canada Cataloguing in Publication

Title: Don't waste your food / written by Deborah Chancellor ; illustrated by Diane Ewen.
Other titles: Do not waste your food
Names: Chancellor, Deborah, author. | Ewen, Diane (Illustrator), illustrator.
Description: Series statement: Good to be green | Previously published: London: Wayland, 2019. | "A story about why it's important not to waste food". | Includes index.
Identifiers: Canadiana (print) 20190194286 | Canadiana (ebook) 20190194294 | ISBN 9780778772811 (hardcover) | ISBN 9780778772880 (softcover) | ISBN 9781427124692 (HTML)
Subjects: LCSH: Food waste—Environmental aspects—Juvenile literature. | LCSH: Food waste—Prevention—Juvenile literature. | LCSH: Sustainable living—Juvenile literature. | LCSH: Environmentalism—Juvenile literature.
Classification: LCC TD804 .C53 2020 | DDC j363.72/88—dc23

Library of Congress Cataloging-in-Publication Data

Names: Chancellor, Deborah, author. | Ewen, Diane (Illustrator), illustrator.
Title: Don't waste your food / written by Deborah Chancellor ; illustrated by Diane Ewen.
Description: New York : Crabtree Publishing Company, 2020. | Series: Good to be green | First published in Great Britain in 2019 by Wayland.
Identifiers: LCCN 2019043447 (print) | LCCN 2019043448 (ebook) | ISBN 9780778772811 (hardcover) | ISBN 9780778772880 (paperback) | ISBN 9781427124692 (ebook)
Subjects: LCSH: Food waste--Prevention--Juvenile literature. | Food waste--Environmental aspects--Juvenile literature. | Food consumption--Juvenile literature. | Waste (Economics)--Juvenile literature.
Classification: LCC HD9000.5 .C465 2020 (print) | LCC HD9000.5 (ebook) | DDC 363.72/8--dc23
LC record available at https://lccn.loc.gov/2019043447
LC ebook record available at https://lccn.loc.gov/2019043448

Don't Waste Your Food

A story about why it's important not to waste food.

Amara wasn't feeling very hungry.
She played with the food on her plate.
"I've had enough to eat!" she said.
Then she pushed the plate away.

Dad looked sad. "Try not to waste your food," he said.

He put some of Amara's leftovers
in the fridge and scraped the rest
into the food compost container.

The next day, Dad made a big breakfast.
"Mmmm, this is delicious!" said Amara.
"Some of your dinner was too good to
throw away," said Dad. "So I used the
leftovers to make an omelette."

"What happened to
the rest of my dinner?"
asked Amara.

Dad showed Amara the garden
composter. "Food scraps make great
fertilizer for my vegetable patch," he said.

"If you put food waste into a composter, it breaks down to make a natural fertilizer," Dad said. "We can compost all our leftovers except meat, fish, dairy food, grease, and oils. These attract pests and smell really bad."

These foods can go in the garden composter to make **fertilizer**.

Don't put these foods in the garden composter!

That evening Amara ate all her dinner.
"What happens to the food people
throw away?" she asked Dad.
"Food is buried in garbage dumps
called landfill sites," Dad said.

That didn't sound good to Amara.

When we throw food away, we also waste the **energy**, water, and **packaging** that was used to transport it to stores. Food in **landfill sites** rots and lets off **methane**, a gas that adds to **global warming**.

"Cheer up!" said Dad.
He got a pen and some paper.
"Let's plan our meals so we
don't buy too much food."
They wrote a shopping list together.

Around the world, about a third
of all the food that is made
for people to eat gets thrown
away. To cut down on waste,
we should not buy more food
than we can eat.

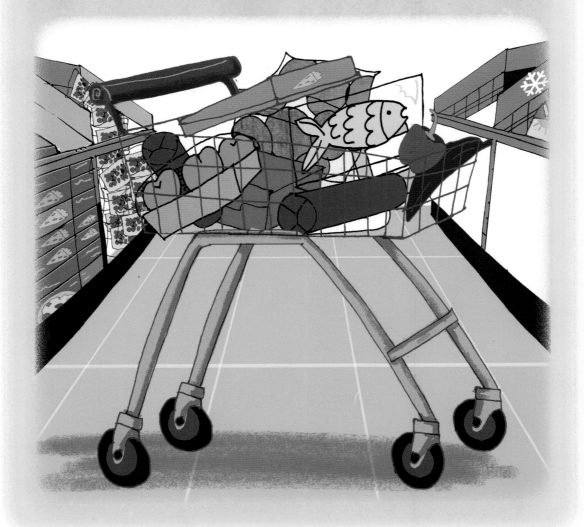

The next day Amara and Dad went to the local market. Amara stopped at her favorite stall.

"Fruit and vegetables are good for you," said Dad. "They give you **vitamins** and **minerals** to keep you healthy."

"Let's buy some apples," said Dad.
"These ones come from a local farm
and are tasty at this time of year."
"Can we get a pineapple too?" asked Amara.
"Maybe next time," said Dad. "Those
pineapples traveled a long way to get here."

Transporting food from a great distance uses up **fuel** and causes air **pollution**. It is better for the **environment** to buy food that is grown close by because it does not need to be shipped far.

Amara checked the shopping list. "We've got more vegetables to buy, because we're eating less meat this week," she said.

Dad picked out some carrots. "Growing crops uses less energy and creates less pollution than farming animals," he said.

There are 1.5 billion cattle on the planet, and each animal lets off a lot of methane gas every day through burping and farting. Farm animals produce more **greenhouse gases** than all of the world's cars, planes, boats, and trains.

Dad and Amara went home with their shopping.

"No need to use the car," said Dad.

"We're going green!" said Amara.

Pre-cooked meals are wrapped in a lot of packaging that is hard to recycle.

Cooking from scratch uses less packaging. It also tastes great and is better for the planet!

That evening, Amara helped Dad cook dinner.

"You're a great chef!" said Dad.

After that, they cooked together every night.
Amara never left another scrap on her plate.

Quiz time

Which of these things are true? Read the book again to find out!

(Cover up the answers on page 29.)

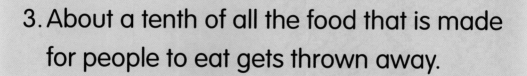

1. Leftovers can be used to help your plants grow.

2. You can put any kind of food in a compost bin.

3. About a tenth of all the food that is made for people to eat gets thrown away.

4. Some food travels around the world before we eat it.

5. Farming animals is good for the planet.

Answers

1. **True**

Leftovers can be used to make compost, which is a good fertilizer for the garden. *(See pages 10–11)*

2. **False**

You can't put meat, fish, dairy foods, oil, or grease into a compost bin because it would attract pests and smell bad. *(See pages 12–13)*

3. **False**

About a third of all the food that is made for people to eat gets thrown away. *(See page 17)*

4. **True**

Some of our food travels around the world instead of coming from a local farm. This uses energy and causes pollution. *(See page 21)*

5. **False**

Cows let off a gas called methane, that contributes to the problem of global warming. *(See page 23)*

Get active

In the story, Amara and Dad plan the meals they are going to eat. They write a shopping list, so they don't buy more food than they need to. Talk to the person who cooks at your home and ask if you can help plan your meals for the next few days. Maybe you could try not eating meat or only eating locally grown or raised foods for a day or a week. What food will you need to buy? Write a shopping list together.

Make a poster about composting, using pictures from magazines. Show what compost is for, and how to make it. Illustrate which kinds of food can be used to make compost, and which kinds of food you can't use.

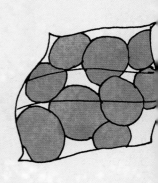

Go to a supermarket and see how many special offers you can find, such as "buy two for the price of one." Make a list of these offers. Talk with an adult about supermarket deals like this. How might they add to the problem of food waste?

Go shopping and find some fruit or vegetables that were grown in a different country. Figure out out how far that fruit traveled to get to the store. Write a story or a poem about the journey that the food took.

A note about sharing this book

The *Good to Be Green* series provides a starting point for further discussion on important environmental issues, such as pollution, climate change, and endangered wildlife. Each topic is relevant to both children and adults.

Don't Waste Your Food!

This story explores some issues surrounding food waste. *Don't Waste Your Food!* contains practical suggestions for how to reduce food waste, such as by planning meals in advance, composting, and writing shopping lists. The information panels in the book also cover the wider issue of global warming and some of its causes, such as methane emissions from food waste in landfills, and dairy farming. The book also considers the environmental impact of global food transportation.

The story and nonfiction elements in *Don't Waste Your Food!* encourage the reader to conclude that we should all try to stop wasting food. One important way to do this is to shop more thoughtfully in the first place.

How to use the book

Adults can share this book with children individually or in small and large groups. The book serves as a starting point for discussion about food waste. Engaging illustrations support the story to raise confidence in children who are starting to read on their own.

The story introduces vocabulary relevant to the theme of food waste, such as: *composters, crops, energy, environment, fertilizer, fuel, global warming, greenhouse gas, landfill site, market, methane, pollution,* and *waste*. Some of the vocabulary in the story and information panels will be unfamiliar to the reader. These words are in bold text, and they are defined in the glossary on page 32. When reading the story for the first time, refer to the glossary with the children.

There is also an index on page 32. Encourage children to use the index when you are talking about the book. For example, ask them to use the index to find the pages that describe landfill sites (pages 14 and 15). This useful research skill can teach children that information can be found in books as well as searched for on the Internet, with a responsible adult.

Glossary

composter A container used to hold fertilizer made of rotting plants and natural materials

energy Power used to make something work

environment The world around us

fertilizer A mixture added to soil to make plants grow more easily

fuel Material (such as gas or oil) burned for heat or power

global warming The rising temperature of Earth's surface, caused by air pollution

greenhouse gases Gases that trap the Sun's rays and warm up Earth, causing Earth's climate to change

landfill sites Places where garbage is buried in the ground

methane One of the greenhouse gases that causes global warming

minerals Nutrients that help you grow and stay well

packaging Materials used to wrap and protect the things we buy

pollution Harmful chemicals that make a place or thing dirty

vitamins Nutrients we need to grow and be healthy

Index